Ce
$13.95

E $13.95   90-266
Be   Bernatova, Eva
             The wonder shoes

For Anna

The Wonder Shoes

EVA BERNATOVÁ
Pictures by FIONA MOODIE

FARRAR, STRAUS & GIROUX

NEW YORK

In the midst of mountains and hills, there was a village—not too small and not too large.

And here lived a girl named Emma.

Emma was very lonely.

She was new to the village and none of the children
wanted to play with her.

Emma watched the others play tag and run and jump,
but the more she watched, the sadder she felt.

If only I could make them notice me, she thought, then they'd play with me.

One day a caravan appeared with a huge sign on it that said CIRCUS UMBERTO. "Step right up," the ringmaster called.

All the people in the village went to the show: the grownups, the children, even Emma.

There were so many things to see!

Each act seemed better than the last.

Then a beautiful dancer in red shoes performed and
Emma knew what she had to do.

After the show, Emma found the dancer. The dancer
listened to Emma, and then gave her a pair of red shoes.
They fit perfectly!

"Come on, little one, it's not difficult," the dancer said.
Soon Emma could pirouette like a real ballerina.

Emma walked home carrying her red shoes. She was
very happy. Surely the children would notice her now.

The Circus Umberto traveled on.

That day, Emma danced for the children. But they were
jealous and joked about her red shoes.

Emma didn't give up. She thought and thought, and the
red shoes gleamed as though they wanted to help her.
Finally, she had an idea.

She found the children and called to them, "We'll put on our own circus."

"Why not?" they said. "Yes! Yes!"

Together, they painted and glued and practiced for hours.

Everyone came to see them perform, and the circus was a great success.

Especially because Emma had many new friends.